Juliet
nearly a
Vet

At The Show

REBECCA JOHNSON

Illustrated by Kyla May

Puffin Books

For Megan –

who loved playing pet shops with me
when we were kids. RJx

PUFFIN BOOKS

UK | USA | Canada | Ireland | Australia
India | New Zealand | South Africa | China

Penguin Books is part of the Penguin Random House group of companies
whose addresses can be found at global.penguinrandomhouse.com.

Penguin
Random House
Australia

First published by Penguin Random House, 2013

Text copyright © Rebecca Johnson, 2013
Illustrations copyright © Kyla May Productions, 2013

The moral right of the author has been asserted.

Cover and text design by Karen Scott © Penguin Random House Australia Pty Ltd
Illustrations by © Kyla May Productions
Typeset in New Century Schoolbook
Colour separation by Splitting Image Colour Studio, Clayton, Victoria
Printed and bound in Australia by Griffin Press, an accredited ISO AS/NZS 14001
Environmental Management Systems printer

National Library of Australia Cataloguing-in-Publication entry:

Johnson, Rebecca
At the show/Rebecca Johnson; illustrated by Kyla May

978 0 14 330705 1 (paperback)

A823.4

www.penguin.com.au

FSC
MIX
Paper from
responsible sources
FSC® C009448

Hi! I'm Juliet. I'm ten years old.
And I'm nearly a vet!

I bet you're wondering how someone who is only ten
could nearly be a vet. It's pretty simple really.
My mum's a vet. I watch what she does and
I help out all the time. There's really not that
much to it, you know...

CHAPTER 1

Vets Can Get Very Busy

It's Saturday and I have so much to do.
Mum's going out to the Browns' dairy
this morning to check on a cow that
has cut itself on a fence. Mum always
lets me come on her rounds because
I'm really helpful. Also, it's great
practice for me, being nearly a vet. She
says my friend Chelsea can come, too.

But first, I have to weigh and
measure my guinea pigs to see how
their pregnancies are going. Lulu is
so big and round now, I'm sure she's

almost the size of a dinner plate.
I can't resist racing back inside and
sneaking one out of the kitchen – just
to see. I'm about to pop Lulu onto the
plate when Chelsea appears.

Chelsea's my best friend. She lives
next door.

'Look at this, Chelsea!'

I sit Lulu on the dinner plate.
There is only a tiny amount of white
showing around the edge and the rest
is covered by guinea pig. We burst out
laughing.

'She looks so cute, doesn't she?' coos
Chelsea. 'She's almost a perfect circle.'

'Here's the really cool part.' I gently
take Chelsea's hand and slide it under

Lulu's enormous belly. 'If you rest your hand here, really gently, sometimes you can feel the babies move.'

We sit in silence and wait.

All of a sudden a huge smile spreads across Chelsea's face. She doesn't say anything at all, but her mouth falls open and she gives a little sigh. She loves my guinea pigs just as much as I do.

I pull the stethoscope from my very own Vet Kit and gently place it over Lulu's heart. I nod at my Vet Diary. 'Can you go to Lulu's chart and record that her heartbeat is strong and regular while I pop her on the scales?'

Chelsea carefully fills in the chart. 'How much longer do you think, Juliet?'

I look down at the chart and flip back to when we started recording her pregnancy.

Date	Weight	Girth measurement	Regular heartbeat	Babies born?
26/5	1344g	44cm	Yes	No.
2/6	1350g	45cm	Yes	No, but getting very fat.
9/6	1354g	45.5cm	Yes	No.
16/6	1359g	46cm	Yes	No – but due any day now.

'Guinea pigs are pregnant for about ten weeks, so she's getting very close now. I can't wait.'

As I lift Lulu, Chelsea looks down at the plate. 'Um, aren't they the plates you eat off?'

I shrug. 'I couldn't find an old one. It'll be right when it's washed.'

'Oh, that is gross,' mutters Chelsea.

I see my five-year-old brother Max heading out to join us. As usual, he has a plastic dinosaur in each hand. Max is obsessed with dinosaurs. It's all he can think about. It drives me nuts. The really annoying thing is that he has hundreds of them and I'm always tripping over them in the house, but

Mum just keeps buying him more.

'Maxasaurus,' I say sweetly. I always call him that when I want something. It works every time.

'Yeah?' he says enthusiastically.

I look at his dinosaur. 'Hey, is that a new one? I haven't seen it before.'

Max beams. 'It's a Liopleurodon. It was a large, carnivorous marine reptile that lived during the mid-Jurassic period. It grew to seven metres long and . . .'

'Wow, it's a beauty, isn't it?' I know I have to stop him short or we'll be here for hours.

Max nods eagerly.

Smiling broadly, I pass him the

plate in my hand and casually say,
'Can you pop this in the sink for me?
I'd love to look at all your dinosaurs
a bit later, but right now I'm flat-out
with my vet rounds. '

'Okay,' grins Max, and he wanders
into the house with the plate.

Chelsea shakes her head and
smiles.

'We'd better get a move on,' I say,
putting Lulu back in her little house.
'I still have to weigh and measure
Twiggy and check Curly's ears for
infection. Mum says she wants to
leave at nine.'

'I'd better get dressed then,' Chelsea
says. 'I can't go out like this! I look like

something the cat's dragged in!'

I look at Chelsea's neat plaits, crisp white shirt, ironed jeans and white sneakers. Then I look down at my PJs. They're covered in fur and straw and a bit of mud. I shrug. I'm much too busy looking after animals to worry about what I'm wearing.

After I've finished my rounds, I race into my bedroom to check I have everything I need in my Vet Kit. Mr Brown's daughter, Maisy, has a cat called Shredder that we rescued once and I want to give her a check-up when we get to the dairy.

'Juliet, are you ready yet?' Mum calls from the verandah. 'I'm just going

8

out to pack the car. Chelsea's already
out here waiting for you.'

'Coming.' I snap my Vet Kit shut,
throw on some clothes and race into
the kitchen to grab a quick drink.

Max is lining all of his dinosaurs
up along the kitchen table. Dad is on
his hands and knees looking under the
sink. Towering stacks of plates and
cups surround him.

'What are you doing?' I ask.

Dad puts his finger to his lips. 'Shhh. Don't tell Mum because I know she'll worry, but I think we might have rats in the kitchen. I found hair all over one of the dinner plates. It was disgusting.'

He shudders as he shows me the plate.

I give Max a warning stare.

Max smiles back at me broadly. 'What time will you be home, Juliet?' he says.

'Why?' I ask suspiciously.

'I just need to know how much time I've got to set up my dinosaurs for you to look at, like you said you would. I'm going to write some stuff down about each one to read out to you.'

The car horn toots.

'I'm going to be ages,' I say.

'That's okay,' he beams. 'It's gonna take me ages to set all of them up. There are still three more boxes in my room.'

I groan.

'Remember, not a word to Mum,' whispers Dad. 'I'll find those rats if it's the last thing I do.'

I back out of the kitchen quickly, feeling a tiny bit guilty. Chelsea is already in the back seat waving eagerly for me to hurry up.

On the drive out to the dairy,

Mum tells us some fantastic news.

'Girls, four bantam chickens were brought into the surgery yesterday afternoon. They were found in a chook pen at an empty house. They are very thin and a bit scruffy, but I wondered if you might like to look after them?'

'Really? We can keep them?' I cry. 'Oh, thank you so much, Mum. Now we'll have even **more** animals to practise our skills on!'

I whip out my notepad and look at notes Chelsea made for me on roosters.

ROOSTERS
- Roosters only crow when they see the light.
- Roosters like the sound of their crow echoing in a metal pool.

I'm going to have to do a lot more research on chickens if Chelsea and I are going to have our own to look after.

'Now, you know your father isn't fond of chickens, but because there are no roosters he has agreed you can have them. He will build a pen, but it will be up to you two to look after them.' Mum glances over her shoulder to check we are listening.

I turn to Chelsea excitedly. 'The first thing we'll have to do is give them a bath. They may have lice.'

Chelsea goes a little pale, but if she is going to be a world-famous animal groomer and trainer she'll have to handle this sort of stuff.

'Just remember,' Mum says, 'looking after pets properly is a lot of hard work. Maybe don't go taking too much else on for a while, hey?'

We nod but we're not really listening. We're too busy talking about what we're going to call our fluffy new friends.

CHAPTER 2

Vets Have to Do House Calls

The Browns' dairy farm is huge and has a great big sign over the gate that says 'Windslow Park Stud'. I come here a lot with Mum because she needs my help with all sorts of things, like the time one of the cows had an infected hoof. I had to pass Mum all the instruments while she held its leg up. Mr Brown also has some sheep and a few horses, so there are plenty of animals to learn about.

I have a full page of COW notes in

my notebook from all my visits.

When we get to the house, Maisy is waiting. She is wearing jeans and riding boots and a checked shirt. Maisy is in our class at school, but she doesn't talk to us a lot. She hangs around with a group of girls I don't like very much. They're all a bit mean. As I'm thinking this, Maisy smiles and waves. It's funny how different people can be away from their friends.

We hop out of the car and Maisy comes racing over.

'Let's go and find Shredder,' she says, and leads us over to the hay shed. Sure enough, Shredder is there hunting through the bales for mice.

Maisy sits on a bale and calls her with a 'puss, puss, puss' and Shredder leaps onto her lap. She looks very plump and content and purrs loudly as Maisy tickles her under the chin.

I put my kit down and pull out my stethoscope. Well, it's **actually** my mum's spare stethoscope. It's my birthday soon and it's on my wishlist. After all, to be a real vet I'll definitely need one.

I listen to Shredder's heartbeat and make some notes.

Shredder
Maisy takes good care of her pets.
Cat is shiny and healthy and relaxed.
Heartbeat good and strong.

'Are you riding in the Show next weekend?' Chelsea asks Maisy when I have finished my checks.

Maisy sighs and looks really sad. 'I've never even seen the horse events at the Show. We always have to hang around the Bull Pavilion. I wanted to ride this year because all my friends are, and that's **all** they ever talk about.' She shrugs. 'But they've got such great horses. I asked Dad if I could ride Thunder, his horse, but Dad says he's too old and it would be too much for him.'

I look out through the huge barn doors and down to the paddock below. I can see two horses grazing there.

One of them is very short and very
round.

'What about that little black one?'
I say, pointing.

Maisy laughs. 'Midgie? You've got to
be kidding. He is the most stubborn,
most annoying pony you've ever met.
All he wants to do is eat. I can't make
him do anything, let alone enter him

in the local Show.'

Chelsea and I look at each other. We know what the other is thinking immediately. Best friends can do that.

'We could help you train him and get him ready,' I say.

Chelsea nods and claps her hands.

Maisy considers it for a moment, then shakes her head.

'We only have one week. It would be impossible.'

'We can do it if we all work together,' says Chelsea. 'I've been reading all about grooming dogs – how different could it be? I've already got some great ideas about how we can really make him stand out in the crowd. And, as you can see, Juliet is nearly a vet.'

Chelsea points at my Vet Kit. It's really Dad's old fishing box, but I don't think they need to know that.

'She knows **all** about animals and is really good with them.'

Maisy looks impressed.

'The thing is,' I say, 'Mum's going to have to come and check on that cow until she has the calf, so we could come every day after school.'

Maisy starts to smile. We're obviously very convincing.

'Well . . .' she says, 'let's go and have a look at him.'

As we get closer I see that Maisy

isn't exaggerating. Midgie is very fat, and very dirty. I look at Chelsea. Her smile is fading.

'Well,' I say, brightly. 'This will be fun.' I think I hear Chelsea make a small, high-pitched squeak.

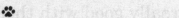

When we get home that afternoon, I see a line of dinosaurs leading from the garage up the front path and in through the front door. Max is sitting on the top step waiting for me. When is Mum going to realise there is something wrong with my brother!

I roll my eyes and bend to pick up the first dinosaur. This is going to be a very long afternoon.

CHAPTER
3

Vets Need to Do Research

I can see I am going to be very busy
looking after all of my animals now.
I have Curly, our dog, Twiggy and
Lulu, my pregnant guinea pigs, our
four new chooks and I'm in charge of
Midgie's food and health schedule.
Being a vet can be exhausting!

We only have one week until
the Show and there is so much to
do. Chelsea and I meet later that
afternoon after I've looked at **all** of
Max's dinosaurs. We put a tick next to

all the events in the Show's schedule that Maisy and Midgie can enter. I make a few notes. I am going to have to plan the perfect diet if Midgie is going to perform at his best.

Best Groomed: An event where cleanliness, dress and neatness is judged and nothing else.

Dressage Test: For ponies 14.2 hands and under.

Best-Educated Hack (under 14 hands class):
An event where the education of the horse counts, not how it looks. Manners and paces are considered, along with how the horse responds to the rider's aids.

Barrel Race: An event in which a horse and rider attempt to complete a clover-leaf pattern around barrels in the fastest time.

Finish - Start

Games on Horseback: Games include musical chairs, bending, flag race, egg-and-spoon race. Requires a fast but agile horse with good steering and brakes.

'But how can a pony have fourteen hands?' says Chelsea. 'That must be a mistake!'

'It's how they measure horses,' I laugh. 'It's how many hands from the top of the horse's shoulder to the ground. They used to measure horses like that in the olden days when they had nothing else to measure them with.'

I stand up from the kitchen table and stretch. 'Hey, Mum's doing an operation in her surgery on a cat tonight. Apparently it's been in a fight and has a nasty big sore on its neck that's got **really** infected. Do you want to come and watch?'

'Um, not really. I can't, I'm sorry,' stammers Chelsea. 'I have to work on my maths.'

I shrug my shoulders. Fancy choosing maths over an operation! I can't wait. Mum says I can help with the bandages and things. It's very cool having a vet surgery in your own backyard.

❖

The next morning is Sunday. After I've finished my rounds, Mum drops us back out at the dairy. Mrs Brown says we can stay all day.

The first thing we need to do is catch Midgie. He lets us get really close, but the minute he sees the rope

we're going to tie around his neck,
he takes off to the far corner of the
paddock.

'I knew this would be useless,' sighs
Maisy. 'He's a total pain.'

But Chelsea and I are not about to
give up so easily.

I race back to the dairy and get
some hay. Ignoring Midgie, I walk

straight over to Thunder and offer him
some, then I casually walk into the
small fenced yard, tie the rope to the
end of the gate and drop the hay on
the ground.

'Come on,' I call to Chelsea and
Maisy. 'Make it look like the only horse
you care about is Thunder.'

They catch on straightaway.

Thunder happily follows the girls
into the yard as they coo and pat him
and feed him more hay.

Midgie watches from a distance and
stamps his foot.

'Now, you guys go into the hay shed
and I'll hide here behind this trough
and pull the gate shut with the rope.'

It only takes a few minutes for the Shetland pony to trot into the yard and make a beeline for the hay. He thinks he's won, until I slam the gate shut behind him.

'YAY,' cheer Chelsea and Maisy from the hay shed.

'See,' says Chelsea, 'I told you Juliet would know exactly what to do. She really is nearly a vet.'

CHAPTER 4

Vets Need to be Able to Outsmart Animals

First we wash Midgie. He has a long shaggy coat that is filthy. I get a little carried away with the horse shampoo Mum has given me. He foams up so much he looks a like a huge woolly sheep.

After we rinse him, Chelsea combs and trims his mane and tail while I check his heartbeat, his teeth for wear, and his hooves for splits and cracks. He is already starting to look like a champion, shining like a new car in the sun. He munches happily on the special grain I have put in his feed bin.

'Time to start his training,' says Chelsea as Maisy carries her saddle to the yard and plonks it down.

Midgie doesn't look impressed as we put the cloth and saddle on his back. We put his bridle on and hold him as Maisy climbs on. She looks very professional in her helmet and boots.

She kicks Midgie gently.

He doesn't move.

She clicks her tongue and whistles.

He stands still and stamps his foot.

'I told you. He's stubborn and useless,' Maisy sighs.

I block Midgie's ears so he doesn't hear what she is saying. 'Perhaps he just doesn't understand,' I say. 'Here, I'll pull him while you kick.'

But Midgie digs his hooves in.

Chelsea steps forward. 'I've got

an idea. They train dogs using food. Maybe it works for ponies too,' she says, holding some hay out in front of the fat pony.

He immediately steps forward.

'Well, it's a start,' I grin as we follow Chelsea and the hay into the paddock.

An hour later, Midgie has sort of practised the barrel race, as well as trotting and cantering in big circles. I think he could keep going, but Chelsea looks like she's going to collapse. She's been running in front of him with hay the entire time.

'I wish you were allowed to do that at the Show,' laughs Maisy as we take off his saddle and brush him down.

Chelsea groans and drops to the ground.

We spend the rest of the day exploring the farm, playing hide and seek, and making a cubby out of hay bales in the hay shed. It's the first time I've ever seen Chelsea's hair look messy, but it's such fun that she doesn't even realise!

Maisy is really funny and shows us all the great things to do on her farm. She's so different here. At school she just giggles and whispers with her friends.

At the end of the day we agree to meet up before school the next morning to work out our schedule for the week.

When we arrive at school, Maisy comes running over with photos of a show horse that she's cut out of a magazine. We all look at it and talk about what we could do to Midgie to make him look that smart.

'And look down here at this photo,' Maisy points. 'Look at his beautiful rug! They put them on the horses for them to travel in so their coat doesn't get dirty.'

'My mum might sew one for us,' beams Chelsea. 'How hard can it be to make a horse rug?'

❖

That afternoon we go with Mum back out to the farm.

Midgie still won't move without food in front of him, but Chelsea is getting faster and puffing less. I reckon she could win the barrel race herself now.

Maisy turns to me. 'Maybe you could ride Thunder in front of Midgie?' she says. 'Perhaps he'll follow.'

'Um . . .' I don't know what to say. I hate riding horses. I had a fall once and got a really bad fright, but I don't really want to tell Maisy that. Vets don't have to be able to ride horses, you know.

Chelsea sees my face and quickly steps in. 'I can ride a bit,' she says.

It works. Midgie is very happy to follow Thunder and they all trot

around the paddock while I get busy
making a list of the things we will
need for the Show. After all, it's only
six days away.

2 buckets – one for food and one for water
a variety of grains and pellets
brushes
combs   rope
hoof pick   rug
saddle cloth   hoof black
saddle   elastics
bridle   helmet
halter   food for us

Chelsea rides over to the fence to
see what I am writing.

'What's hoof black?' she asks.

'It's special paint they put on horses'
hooves to make them look shiny for

shows. I read about it on the internet. It's expensive though.'

'My dad's got heaps of paint. I'll see what's in his shed,' says Chelsea.

Maisy comes over. 'Are you sure you don't want a ride, Juliet?'

'Umm . . . I'd love to, but I just don't have time, sorry. I've really got to plan out what Midgie's diet should be for the next week.'

'Oh, of course,' says Maisy. 'Come on, Chelsea, I'll show you the creek.'

As they ride off I look down at my notepad and try to concentrate on the list I am making. Chelsea is bouncing around so much on Thunder's back that I'm sure she's going to fall off, but

I can hear her laughing.

I smile, too, but I get a funny feeling in my stomach. When we first started hanging out with Maisy it was great, but now I'm not so sure. Chelsea and Maisy seem to be having lots of fun together.

I hope Mum will come and get us soon.

CHAPTER 5

Vets Can Feel Left Out, Too

On the ride home in the car, I don't really feel like talking. I think I'm really tired. Chelsea's telling Mum all about how she rode Thunder and how she even rode Midgie. Mum seems pretty impressed.

I pretend I'm busy making more notes in my book.

Chelsea goes home and doesn't come back to help with my afternoon rounds, but I don't really mind.

❖

The next day Chelsea comes over to walk to school with me. She tells me about how Maisy rang her to discuss what the horse rug should look like because Chelsea's mum has agreed to sew it. They are going to make it out of some old curtains or something.

'Are you okay?' she asks, when I don't really say much.

'I've just got a bit of a headache,' I shrug.

Maisy is excited when she catches us just outside the school gates. She tells us that this morning she got up early and rode Midgie around the paddock without Thunder and without food! She really is working hard to get

41

him ready for the big day.

'That's great,' I say. 'Will you practise all your events every day after school this week? He has to perform like a champion as well as look great.'

We all chat excitedly for a few more minutes. I know one of the cows has some stitches in its leg that Mum needs to check, so we agree to meet back at Maisy's farm on Thursday after school. Only five days to go until the Show, but things are looking good!

❖

That afternoon I don't go next door to Chelsea's. I want to help Dad. He's building a chook pen in our backyard for our new chooks to live in. It is very nice of Dad to do this, because he doesn't like animals very much. I still think it's pretty funny that he married a vet!

Chelsea and I have decided to call our chooks Muffin, Pikelet, Cream Puff and Cupcake. They are so cute and the names suit them perfectly because they love their food. They are scruffy little bantams in a mixture of colours.

Muffin is a black Silkie bantam, which means her feathers are more like fluff. Pikelet, Cream Puff and Cupcake are called Frizzle bantams and their feathers all curl backwards so they are really puffy-looking.

They even have feathers on their feet!

Dad's an architect, so he's designed the coolest chook pen you've ever seen. I've drawn it in my notepad so I can show my teacher at school.

The Coolest Chook Pen Ever!

Dad says he wants to make it very secure, so he builds a really high fence around it.

'Is that to stop dogs and cats from getting in?' I ask, impressed.

'No,' says Dad, 'it's to stop the chooks getting out and pooping all over the verandah.'

Now it makes sense why he is going to so much trouble!

'You don't have to worry, Dad,' I reassure him. 'I'm nearly a vet, you know. I'll take care of everything.'

Dad shudders a bit. I hope he's not remembering the little problem we had not so long ago with escaped rats and roosters crowing at dawn.

CHAPTER
6

Vets Need Lots of Different Skills

When Mum and I arrive on Thursday afternoon, Maisy and Chelsea are already down in the paddock with Thunder and Midgie practising the events. They've found a few old barrels in the shed and they're trotting around them – although Midgie keeps veering off to munch on clumps of grass or daisies. It looks like fun.

'You'll definitely have a chance in the events now,' I call out.

Maisy smiles, but she doesn't look convinced.

'People take these shows really seriously, you know,' she says. 'Maybe we should all just go and watch.'

'No way!' I cry. 'You've got the perfect team here. I'm nearly a vet, Chelsea's nearly a famous animal groomer, Midgie's nearly a horse, and you're nearly about to win a blue ribbon.'

Maisy laughs and looks down at Midgie. She pats his neck. 'Come on,' she says. 'Let's go and have a drink.'

❖

The next morning the chook pen is ready. I've already weighed each of the bantams and checked their claws, feathers and beaks for any signs of disease.

Name	Beak	Weight	General condition	Eggs laid
Cream Puff	Good	1.1kg	Feathers dull. Flaky skin. Will need to bath and check for mites. Needs to gain weight.	No
Muffin	Small chip on top. Not serious.	1kg	Very thin. Also needs a bath.	No
Cupcake	Good	1.2kg	In better condition than the others. Needs a bath.	No
Pikelet	Crack along bottom edge. Will need to show it to Mum.	950g	Smallest chook by far. Not as active. Needs a lot of care.	No

Max is sitting in the new pen with me. For once he isn't holding a dinosaur.

'Did you know, Max . . .' I say, happy to have an audience because I've been reading Mum's textbook on chickens. 'You can tell if a chicken is healthy by the comb on its head.' I bring Cupcake a little closer so that he can examine the fleshy red skin on the top of the chook's head. 'If it's limp it means the chook is unwell.'

'Wow,' says Max, touching the comb. 'It's a bit like the frill around a Triceratops' neck, only softer.'

'How do you manage to make everything about dinosaurs?' I groan.

But secretly I'm quite amazed that he knows so many facts, even if they are useless ones about dinosaurs.

❖

It's Saturday. The day of the Show is suddenly here. We have done everything we can to get ready. Chelsea's mum is putting the final touches on the rug for Midgie to travel in, I have his meals for the day organised and my Vet Kit for a last-minute check-up, and Maisy has been working hard training Midgie all week.

My alarm wakes me at five a.m. Sometimes vets need to get up really early.

I see the lights on next door.

Chelsea must be up, too. I creep out
the back door to do my rounds. The
chooks are very happy to see me and
come rushing over for their breakfast.

I notice the guinea pigs haven't
eaten any of their food from last night
and suddenly I'm worried. Are they all
right? I lift the lid of their cage and
catch my breath.

'They're here, they're here!' I yell
as I run inside and up the stairs, not
caring that it's five in the morning.
Who wouldn't want to know my news?

I race into Mum and Dad's bedroom
and leap onto their bed.

'Twiggy and Lulu have BOTH had
their babies!' I yell.

Mum laughs. 'Oh how lovely,
darling. How many are there?'

I stop to think. 'HEAPS! I haven't
counted them yet. Will you come and
see? Will you check they are all okay?'

'Yay,' says Dad as he hits me
with a pillow. 'Just what I've always
wanted . . . **heaps** more guinea pigs!'

I laugh and roll off the bed.

Then I race back outside and scoot across the lawn. Mrs O'Sullivan is doing Chelsea's hair in the kitchen.

'They're here,' I yell over the fence. 'Twiggy and Lulu have both had their babies!'

Chelsea leaps off the chair with her hair half brushed and bursts out the back door.

Mum is leaning over the cage. As the sun's first rays light up our backyard, we look down on my **nine** new baby guinea pigs. I grin at Chelsea and she grins back. It's going to be a glorious day!

I race back to my room to pack my Vet Kit and notebook and get changed. I rummage through the pile of clothes on the floor and pull on my jeans and look for a shirt.

'We've got to go, Juliet,' Mum's voice calls from the front door as I shove a piece of toast into my mouth. I can't be late today. Mum is the vet on duty at the Show.

As we drive to the dairy, Chelsea and I make a list of possible guinea pig names. We don't know if they are boys or girls yet, because Mum said it would be a good idea to leave them for a day to get settled in before we touched them.

Possible boy GP names	Possible girl GP names
	Lavender
Rufus	Rosemary
Spike	Clover
Scruffy	Ginger
Chubby	

CHAPTER 7

Vets are Busy at Shows

When we get to the Browns' dairy, we leap out of the car and run over to Maisy. She has Midgie tied up to her Dad's old horse float and is brushing him. He looks great.

'Maisy, we've got **nine** baby guinea pigs!'

We all dance around happily for a moment, but then we have to get to work. We're running behind schedule because of all the excitement.

'Have you got the hoof black and

the rug?' I ask Chelsea.

'Sure do,' she says, grabbing a very large bag from the back of Mum's car.

'Now I know you said "hoof black", but Dad didn't have any black paint so can it be "hoof blue"? I think it could look really cool.'

She holds up a can of bright blue paint.

Chelsea and I start laughing.

'Well, I guess new fashion has to start somewhere,' says Maisy, but she seems a little unsure.

We paint Midgie's hooves and put on his new rug. Chelsea's mum has gone to a heap of trouble. She's used one of Chelsea's brother's old curtains

from when he went through his fluoro
phase. The blue, purple and orange
swirls match Midgie's hooves perfectly.

'Now for the finishing touches,' says
Chelsea as she ties a large blue bow
around his forelock (that's his fringe)
and some pom poms at the top of
his tail.

Midgie looks gorgeous. We definitely have a very good chance of winning something in the grooming event at least – especially if they give marks for creativity.

Mr Brown comes over to help us load Midgie and all his belongings into the float. He looks quite surprised when he sees Midgie.

Mum gives Mr Brown a big smile. 'Doesn't he look . . . bright!'

'Mmm. Very,' nods Mr Brown.

Mum drives us because Mr and Mrs Brown have to take their prize bull in the truck. As we head towards the Show, I run Maisy through some horse-handling tips on the way.

I've never been to a horse event before. The first things I notice as we pull up are all the fancy new horse floats with beautiful, shiny horses tied to them. Their manes are plaited into little knobs all down their necks and their tails are magnificent. Some of them even have checkerboard shapes combed into their rumps. None of them have pom poms or bows. Although I do see a poodle with some.

The girls and boys are all wearing the same clothes – black coats, cream leggings (I find out later that they are called 'jodhpurs') and long black riding boots. I didn't realise you had to wear a uniform.

I look over at Maisy. She is looking down at her jeans and blue shirt.

'I don't think I can do this,' she whispers.

'Of course you can! We'll do it together. You've worked too hard to not try,' says Chelsea, putting her arm around Maisy's shoulder.

Maisy smiles. Briefly.

I feel a little flicker of something not very nice in my stomach when Maisy gives Chelsea a big hug.

As we unload Midgie, a hush falls over the riders and their parents. They are obviously all incredibly impressed with how beautiful Midgie looks. I can see some of them whispering behind their hands. No doubt they are wondering where we bought our 'hoof blue'. Their rugs are so boring. Ours radiates with colour. I recognise Porsha, Maisy's friend from school. I wave and smile but she doesn't wave back. Maybe she didn't see me?

All the stables are already full, so we look for somewhere to tie Midgie up.

'What about the tent post at the back of that stall?' I suggest. 'It's in the shade and right near a tap, so we can fill his water bucket.'

'Juliet, you're full of good ideas,' beams Chelsea.

I mix up Midgie's 'calming' food for the first events and he munches away happily. I read on the internet that grassy hay is best for this and Mr Brown had plenty in his barn.

I look at my watch. 'We still have a bit of time before your first event, Maisy. Want to have a look around?'

I think Maisy is glad to have a distraction. She looks a bit nervous.

We decide to visit the Bull Pavilion.

We find Mr Brown grooming his best friesian bull, Ramadan Windslow the Third. He looks fantastic.

Mr Brown says the judging will be just before lunch and we promise to be back to watch it. I glance over at the other bulls in the stalls and feel quite confident that Ramadan has an excellent chance because of his massive size and strong neck.

'We'd better start heading back,' says Chelsea. 'They'll call the first event soon.'

CHAPTER
8
Crunch Time

We sprint back to the main arena
to get Midgie ready for his first
event, 'Best Groomed'. As we round
the corner, I realise we might have
a problem. I guess we should have
checked to see what kind of stall we
had tied Midgie up to.

Who knew horses would like toffee
apples?

'Oh dear,' says Chelsea as we
look at pieces of chewed stick on the
ground.

Midgie's lips are red and sticky. It almost looks like he has lipstick on. He has obviously stuck his head under the back of the tent and helped himself to the apples that were sitting on a crate as the toffee dried.

I put my finger to my lips as we quietly untie Midgie and slip away before the owners of the stall figure out where all their apples have gone.

'Oh Midgie,' scolds Maisy. 'You are such a pig. How are you going to run now?'

We throw his saddle onto his back and try to tidy him up. Even though he must have just eaten at least twenty toffee apples, he still keeps ducking his head down to eat grass. As Maisy rides him out into the ring, I can't help

noticing the dry grass that's stuck all over his lips. It makes him look like he's swallowed a cactus.

At first, all the horses walk around in a slow circle with the judges standing in the middle of the ring. One at a time they call each horse into the centre and inspect it carefully. Midgie is still circling. He hasn't been called yet.

'Looks like they are leaving the best until last,' I say, nudging Chelsea.

Then something very odd happens.

The judges tie beautiful, long, shiny ribbons around some of the horse's necks. Porsha smiles primly. Her horse is wearing a blue ribbon. She has won first place. I gasp. But they haven't even looked at Midgie!

Everyone slowly leaves the arena.

Porsha leans towards Maisy as she is trotting past and says something. Then she laughs.

Maisy slowly walks Midgie over to us. I can see she is trying not to cry.

'They're all laughing at me. Porsha said Midgie looks ridiculous and the Show is an event for real horses and I should go home before I make a fool of myself.'

I turn and look around. Porsha and a group of girls, some of them from school, are in a huddle a little way off, whispering and giggling. When they see me looking they all pretend to be looking at the ground.

How stupid do they think we are?

'I can't go out there again,' says Maisy. 'I want to go home.' She looks around for her dad.

'Maisy, listen to me,' I say as we walk over to the bull judging. 'We've made a mistake. I can see that these judges don't value creativity, but between us we have more courage than any of those girls put together. *We* saved Shredder. *We* got Midgie ready ourselves without any help from anyone else.'

I point behind me at all the parents fussing over the horses while the girls stand around talking about us. 'We came here to do a job and we have to finish it. You can do this, Maisy! Ignore them all.'

Maisy tries to smile. 'I guess Midgie does look like he's going to a disco,' she murmurs. Then she starts giggling.

Chelsea and I look at each other in relief. Then we all start laughing so hard we can't stop.

When we finally get to the bull judging, we see Mr Brown's bull with a Grand Champion sash around his neck. It's three times as wide and twice as long as Porsha's ribbon! We cheer excitedly and drape it around Maisy's neck.

The next event on the schedule for Midgie is the 'Best Girl Rider' class. The girls on their beautiful, tall horses trot around the judges in a large steady circle. Their bottoms rise and fall into the saddles without a sound. Because Midgie is smaller, he trots a lot more quickly. As Maisy uses her stirrups to try to rise and fall in time with his quick pace her saddle squeaks. It makes quite a good beat. Pfft, pfft, squeak, pfft, pfft, squeak.

Everything is going well until Midgie starts cutting across the middle of the circle. At first I think Maisy is doing it to give the judges a closer look at her skills. It is only when one of the judges has to leap clear that I realise that Midgie is just trying to take a few shortcuts.

Yet again Midgie comes away from the ring without a ribbon. Porsha wins, of course, and rides past Maisy with her nose in the air.

'Don't worry,' I reassure Maisy as I pour oats into Midgie's feed bin. 'That's it for the formal events. The next ones are all about speed, so you'll be fine.'

Chelsea nods in agreement as she removes the pom poms from Midgie's tail. 'We don't want anything to slow him down,' she says.

Maisy told us that flag races are timed. The goal is to see how quickly the rider can turn their horse around a series of poles with flags in them. As they round each pole the rider collects the flag and returns it to a bucket at the start. Midgie was very good at this when we practised on the farm. He can turn sharply and he isn't afraid of the bright flags flapping in the breeze.

Maisy's face is a picture of concentration as the hooter goes off.

She kicks Midgie and they gallop towards the pole. Midgie turns, right on time. Maisy leans forward and grabs the flag. Then she races back to the bucket. Chelsea and I are going crazy as he bolts for the second and then the third flag. The judges hold their stopwatches in front of them at the finish line. This is going to be a brilliant time. Midgie gallops straight for flag number four.

Suddenly there is an all-too-familiar

sound. Pellets being poured into a
metal bucket. Midgie's ears flicker.
I can tell he is trying to resist, but he
can't help himself. He runs straight
past the flag towards the fence where
Porsha stands shaking a food bin.

'Oops,' she smiles as Midgie runs to

the fence expectantly.

Maisy isn't sad or embarrassed anymore. She's angry. Really angry. I think a lot of people are. Porsha's mum comes over and tells Porsha to go back to their horse float and before we can say anything she disappears into the crowd.

We gloomily walk back to the stall. Chelsea sneaks me a look. Neither of us knows what to say. Maybe Maisy was right. Maybe this isn't the sort of place for us. It's nearly over and I'm quite glad.

CHAPTER 9

It's Showtime

Then the loudspeaker calls for the last
event of the day. It's the Barrel Race.

'You don't have to do it if you're
tired, Maisy,' I say.

'This is Porsha's favourite event,'
she says grimly, and she turns Midgie
towards the ring and trots in. Porsha
looks surprised to see her, but Maisy
doesn't even look at her. She just sits
up tall and faces the judges.

'How's she going?'

I turn to see Max mounted on top

of his huge inflatable Tyrannosaurus. He's made a bridle for it out of string.

'Oh, great,' I say. 'Now the circus really has come to town.'

Max looks around excitedly.

'A circus?'

I sigh. 'Where's Dad? Did he bring you?'

'He's just over there with Mum. Some horse has cut its leg in the jumping so she has to fix it up. There's gore everywhere. It's disgusting.'

For a moment I am torn. I would love to go and help Mum, but I know I have to stay and support Maisy.

One by one, the horses and their riders come forward to compete in the barrel race. Some of the horses are dancing around, almost bursting with excitement. When it comes to their turn, they are all amazingly fast. I look over at Midgie and Maisy. He is quietly eating some grass. We are doomed.

Then I have an idea.

'Chelsea. Grab a bucket. Here, put this in it.' I grab a handful of pellets and throw them into it. Then I put some in mine. I whisper my plan in her ear and we race into our positions, just in time. Midgie is up next.

Maisy struggles to get him to lift his head from eating the grass. Porsha laughs out loud. I glare at her.

'Hey, Midgie!' I call loudly, and I shake the bucket of pellets. I stand on the other side of the fence, right behind the first barrel.

Midgie looks up straightaway. He starts to prance on the spot as Maisy edges towards the starting line. She holds him back with her reins.

'Go!' says the timekeeper.

Midgie races towards me. All Maisy can do is hang on. As he gets to the barrel I run away from the fence and Chelsea takes over from the other side of the arena. He spins and races around the first barrel perfectly.

'Midgie!' screams Chelsea, furiously shaking her bucket.

The little pony is so excited he takes off towards the other side of the arena. Maisy is onto it now. She holds on with all her might and spins him hard at the second barrel.

By now I am in position at the third. If we can just get him to this side, all Maisy has to do is race him back to the finish line. He races towards me and stops dead at the fence, waiting for his food. One second, two seconds . . . but Maisy can't turn him around.

BOOM!

Max's inflatable dinosaur bursts behind us. The noise is unbelievable.

Midgie spins around and takes off like a shot. Maisy hangs on for dear life.

Midgie crosses the finish line and keeps running all the way to the back of the arena where Chelsea is waiting with his food.

The whole place is quiet, except for the soft sobs of poor Max behind me.

The judge and timekeeper look at

each other and shrug, before writing
down the time.

Maisy proudly leaves the arena with
a long, shiny green ribbon tied around
Midgie's neck. We all hug each other,
and then we hug Max. I'm sure Dad
can fix his dinosaur.

'Well, it's not blue, but it's definitely
a ribbon,' I grin.

'Oh, but don't you know?' says
Maisy, kissing the ribbon. 'Green is my
favourite colour in the whole world!'

A couple of Maisy's friends from school cheer as she leaves the arena. Then they come over to see us. Porsha calls out to them, but they don't seem to hear her.

While Maisy gets her photograph taken, Chelsea and I start brushing down Midgie.

I look at Chelsea.

'You know how I was quiet the other day and I said it was because I had a headache?'

Chelsea looks at me.

'Well, the reason I was quiet was that I was scared that you were starting to like Maisy better than me.'

Chelsea drops her brush.

'Juliet Fletcher! I like Maisy, I really do. But just because I like her doesn't mean I am going to like you less or leave you out. I *know* how awful that feels. If we all stick together, we might even show some of those girls at school how much fun you can have without having to be part of a group.'

Chelsea grins at me as Maisy comes to join us, and I suddenly feel really, really happy.

As we drive off that afternoon we look back at Midgie through the windows of the horse float trailing behind us. He looks very smart with his green ribbon looped around his neck.

And Maisy can't stop smiling.
It's very satisfying being a vet.

Quiz! Are You Nearly a Vet?

1. Why do they paint horses hooves for shows?
   a. To match their handbags.
   b. To make them look shiny and healthy.
   c. So the horse feels more confident.
   d. Because painting their noses doesn't look very good.

2. Which event does Maisy win a ribbon in?
   a. Flag race
   b. Hairiest horse
   c. Best apple eater
   d. Barrel race

3. How many baby guinea pigs are born?
   a. 9
   b. 8
   c. 58
   d. 11

4. Why shouldn't you touch baby guinea pigs when they are first born?
   a. It messes up their hairstyle.
   b. You have to wait until visiting hours.
   c. It can make them sick and their mother may reject them.
   d. They might start calling you 'Mum'.

5. How are the feathers different on frizzle bantams?
   a. They smell like bacon.
   b. They are bright and pink.
   c. They curl backwards.
   d. They fall out if you touch them.

6. What do you call the hair that runs down the top of a horse's neck?
a. A forelock.
b. A mohawk.
c. A fringe.
d. A mane.

7. What did Juliet use to measure the size of the guinea pigs?
a. Max's plastic dinosaur.
b. A tape measure.
c. A dinner plate.
d. Her hand.

8. How can you tell if a chicken is healthy?
a. Its comb on its head is nice and bright and stands up.
b. It doesn't eat too many lollies before dinner.
c. It goes for a 10km jog every day.
d. It eats the carrots first when you throw the scraps out.

9. What do they measure the height of horses in?
a. feet
b. heads
c. hands
d. bananas

10. How do you know when you have a good friend?
a. She cleans your room for you on Saturdays.
b. She writes your name all over her pencil case.
c. She doesn't leave you out when someone new comes along.
d. She names her pet after you.

Answers : 1b, 2d, 3a, 4c, 5c, 6d, 7b, 8a, 9c, 10c. Well done!

. . . . Collect all the Juliet nearly a Vet books!

The Great Pet Plan

My best friend Chelsea and I ♥ animals.
I have a dog Curly and two guinea pigs, but
we need more pets if I'm going to learn to be
a vet. Today, we had the best idea ever...
We're going to have a pet sleepover!

At the Show

Chelsea and I are helping our friend, Maisy,
get her pony ready for the local show. But
Midgie is more interested in eating than in
learning to jump (sigh). Pony training is a bit
more difficult than we thought!

Farm Friends

It's Spring and all the animals on Maisy's farm
are having babies. Maisy says I can stay for a
whole week and help out. There are chicks and
ducklings hatching, orphan lambs to feed, and
I can't wait for Bella to have her calf!

Bush Baby Rescue

A terrible bushfire has struck and Mum's vet
clinic is in chaos. Every day more and more
injured baby animals arrive. Chelsea and I
have never been busier! But who knew that
babies needed so much feeding. I may never
sleep again!

Beach Buddies

It's the holidays and we're going camping by the beach. I can't wait to toast marshmallows by the campfire, swim in the sea and explore the rock pools – there are so many amazing animals at the beach.

Zookeeper for a Day

I've won a competition to be a zookeeper for a day! My best friend Chelsea is coming too. I can't wait to learn all about the zoo animals. There will be meerkats, tigers and penguins to feed. And maybe some zoo vets who need some help (I won't forget my vet kit!).

The Lost Dogs

There was a huge storm last night and now there are lots of lost dogs. One turned up outside my window (he must have known I'm nearly a vet). Luckily, Chelsea, Mum and I are helping out at the Lost Dogs' Home.

Playground Pets

Chelsea and I have such a cool school – we get to have playground pets! Guinea pigs, lizards, fish and insects are all part of our science room. But this week, we have a replacement teacher, and Miss Fine doesn't know much about animals. Luckily we do (it's so handy being nearly a vet).

From Rebecca Johnson

Being a science teacher is the best job for me because I have an excuse to have pets in my class-room. My teaching partner, Caroline, and I have lizards, guinea pigs, stick insects, crayfish and lots more. The thing I like most about this is that all the kids in the school get to share these pets and learn how to look after them properly. My husband loves it too because, for some strange reason, he's not so crazy about too many pets at home...except his horse! And when kids bring injured animals to me for help, I feel a bit like a vet too!

From Kyla May

As a little girl, I always wanted to be a vet. I had mice, guinea pigs, dogs, goldfish, sea snails, sea monkeys and tadpoles as pets. I loved looking after my friend's pets when they went on holidays and every Saturday I helped out at a pet store.
Now that I'm all grown up, I have the best job in the world. I get to draw lots of animals for chil-dren's books and for animated TV shows. In my studio I have two dogs, Jed and Evie, and two cats, Bosco and Kobe, who love to watch me draw.